3

PARTY CRASHERS

BOOK
3

BAD Princesses

PARTY CRASHERS

JENNIFER TORRES

Scholastic Inc.

For Magnus and Vito

Copyright © 2024 by Jennifer Torres

All rights reserved. Published by Scholastic Inc., *Publishers since 1920*. SCHOLASTIC and associated logos are trademarks and/or registered trademarks of Scholastic Inc.

The publisher does not have any control over and does not assume any responsibility for author or third-party websites or their content.

No part of this publication may be reproduced, stored in a retrieval system, or transmitted in any form or by any means, electronic, mechanical, photocopying, recording, or otherwise, without written permission of the publisher. For information regarding permission, write to Scholastic Inc., Attention: Permissions Department, 557 Broadway, New York, NY 10012.

This book is a work of fiction. Names, characters, places, and incidents are either the product of the author's imagination or are used fictitiously, and any resemblance to actual persons, living or dead, business establishments, events, or locales is entirely coincidental.

ISBN 978-1-338-83320-1

10 9 8 7 6 5 4 3 2 1   24 25 26 27 28

Printed in the U.S.A.   40
First printing 2024

Book design by Maeve Norton

CHAPTER 1

Princesa Jacinta, torchlight glowing in her eyes, comes to the end of her story. "And the witch, disguised as an owl, always reveals herself with a long, lonely whistle."

Just then, a high-pitched shriek slices through the darkness.

Everyone screams.

Everyone except Dalia and Dominga.

They have already guessed that the witch

in their midst is actually Princesa Candelaria, crouching at the edge of the campfire circle.

"I wouldn't mind if an owl visited me at night," Dalia whispers to Dominga. They sit just outside the circle, a little apart from the rest of the first-year princesas. "Even if it *was* a witch. Owls have special wings that let them fly silently to swoop down on their prey."

A lizard pokes his head out of the top of Dalia's black boot. He sticks his tongue out.

"Don't worry, Don Ignacio," Dalia says, running a finger over his head. "I'd never let an owl come for *you.*"

Dominga pulls her black velvet cloak tighter around her shoulders. She was hopeful when Profesora Colibrí, the head teacher, announced that their evening at the base of Mount Linda

Vista would end with scary stories around the campfire. It might even make up for the swimming in crystal waters (too refreshing), the roasting of marshmallows (too gooey), and the singing of camp songs (too chirpy) they've already been forced to endure.

"We might as well listen for a while," she had told Dalia. Scary would be a welcome relief from the Fine and Ancient Institute for the Royal's usual sticky-sweetness.

The campfire crackles. Orange-red flames dance inside a ring of stones. Violet sparks leap out and flit toward the stars. Dominga follows them with her eyes, up, up to where the ghostly towers of the Bewitched Academy for the Dreadful rise against the full moon.

That is where Dalia and Dominga truly belong.

They are not royals-in-training like the rest of these princesas. They are villains—secret villains, but villains nonetheless. Yet their hopes of getting into the B.A.D. seem as slim as one of these stories being actually creepy. The B.A.D. is notoriously selective. Only the most truly awful and desperately dangerous students are offered admission.

And so far, Dalia and Dominga have not proven themselves good enough—that is, *bad* enough— to attend. But they have not given up. Villains never do.

"Thank you, Casita Sapphire, for that wonderfully chilling tale," Profesora Colibrí says, applauding. Jacinta and Candelaria curtsy as the rest of the princesas clap. "Ten gems for your chalice." The clapping from Casita Sapphire grows louder. On the first day of school, Profesora Colibrí assigned each new princesa to a cottage: Ruby, Sapphire, Emerald, or Opal. For every noble deed accomplished, a princesa can earn gems for her Casita's chalice. The house with the most gems at the end of the term will earn the privilege of venturing into the village beyond the palace's walls.

"Would Casita Opal like to terrify us next?" Profesora Colibrí asks.

"Not likely," Dominga mutters. Dalia snickers.

"What was that, Princesa?" The profesora leans her ear toward Dominga. "Will you be telling a story on behalf of your Casita?"

Before Dominga can reply, a tall princesa with coppery curls springs to her feet. "Of course not," she says, grabbing the torch from Jacinta. "I've been preparing our story for weeks." Princesa Inés is determined to be named the Fairest of the F.A.I.R., the most perfect of all the princesas, by the time they graduate.

"Of course," Profesora Colibrí says, and settles back into her camp chair.

Dalia gathers up the folds of her satin gown, a green so dark it is almost black. "I think we've stayed long enough, don't you agree?" she whispers.

Dominga pushes her glasses up higher on her nose. *"Too* long," she whispers back. They have a plot to set afoot.

As Inés clears her throat and begins her story, Dalia and Dominga sneak away into the shadows.

Four round tents stand in a line at the edge of the campsite. Silky streamers fly from the tops of each one: red, blue, green, and white. Inside the tents, lanterns twinkle over cushioned cots. A satin sleep mask sits atop every plumped pillow.

Dalia and Dominga scurry past to the smaller, plainer tent, where earlier, they all stored their luggage. Hiking gowns hang from racks, ready to be worn the next day. A day that will no doubt be warm and gold-tinged just like every other day at the F.A.I.R.

Or it would be, Dominga thinks, *if Dalia and I weren't about to roll in like storm clouds.*

The idea came to her when they arrived that afternoon. As the others began unpacking, Dominga swiped a pair of scissors from Valentina, the Ruby princesa who is always busy with some new craft. She wouldn't miss it. She'd packed two more pairs. "One for paper, one for fabric, and one for embroidery," Valentina had explained.

It reminded Dominga of the spoons in Chef

Luís-Esteban's kitchen. The wooden spoon for stirring caramel. The slotted spoon for lifting potatoes out of boiling water. The long-handled ladle for scooping up soup. Not to mention the endless spoons for eating. The kitchen will be one of the few places Dominga misses when she and Dalia finally receive their invitations to the B.A.D.

Which they surely will after this scheme. Never mind that all their others have turned out horribly, disastrously, gruesomely *nice*.

Standing in front of the rack of gowns, Dalia taps on the toe of her boot. Don Ignacio peeks out and tests the air with his tongue.

"Where shall we begin?" Dalia asks the lizard. "You can pick first."

He creeps out of the boot and scurries up one side of the rack, across the rod, and down into the pocket of an amber gown with white choke-cherry blossoms embroidered around the neck.

Dominga can tell without looking at the tag that it belongs to Inés. "Excellent choice," she says.

She takes the scissors out of her pocket and offers them to Dalia. "Would you like to make the first cut?"

Dalia peels off her tattered gloves. "I would be delighted." The blades slice through the bottom of the gown as easily as a knife through lemon cream pie.

Dominga can already imagine the horrified screams when the princesas find their gowns cut in half. The whimpers when brambles poke their knees and thorns tear their stockings on the trail. They'll be so miserable, they'll turn on one another. Think of the bickering!

"Think of the chaos!" she shouts.

Dalia lowers the scissors. Her eyes widen behind a curtain of dark hair.

"Sorry," Dominga says, clapping her hand over her mouth. "I must have gotten ahead of myself."

"Understandable," Dalia replies. "But we don't want to be discovered, not when there are so many gowns to . . . *improve*."

By which she means *destroy*. Dominga takes the scissors and turns to the next gown.

When they are finished, shimmering piles of satin and tulle, silk and velvet drift at their feet.

"Soon, we will be packing our trunks and preparing to leave for the B.A.D.," Dalia says, putting her gloves back on. "This time, I am certain."

She tugs on the pocket of the amber gown.

"We're finished, Don Ignacio," she says. "It's time to return to the campfire before we're missed."

But when she sees his tail hanging out of the top, she grins. "On second thought," she says, "stay exactly where you are."

CHAPTER
2

Buttery beams of sunlight stream through the fine-mesh windows of Casita Opal's tent the next morning. They land on Dominga's nose. She lifts her sleep mask and opens one eye. When they were setting up the campsite, Princesa Leonor positioned one of the crystal lanterns so that it would catch the morning light. Now rainbows are scattered all over the tent's canvas walls. Leave it to a princesa to make a shimmering dawn even more putridly pleasant. Dominga squeezes both eyes shut again and pulls her blanket over her head. She rolls over in her cot.

But just as she is drifting off, the twittering of sparrows in the trees outside rouses her again. "Wake up! Wake up!" they chirp in that relentlessly cheery way of songbirds. "Or you'll miss breakfast." She has studied animal-speak for long enough now that she knows the birds are off to search for insects or to peck away at the cookie crumbs the princesas left sprinkled around the campsite. But there's no need to be so *happy* about it.

Still groggily only half-awake, Dominga begins to dream, and in her dream, the chirps turn into the squeaks of rats scurrying across a cold and dismal dungeon. Much better.

Until there is a scream. And it's not in Dominga's dream. It is outside. If Dominga didn't know any better, she'd say it was a barn owl. But she does know better. Barn owls almost always hunt at night.

She yanks off her sleep mask and sits up on her cot as the scream continues. It's not a bird. It's—

"Inés," Leonor says. She's already maneuvered into her chair with its big off-road wheels, made especially for trails. The gems in her tiara match the rainbow drops of paint that forever speckle her gloves. She opens the tent flap and starts to push through.

Dominga turns to Inés's cot, empty now, her blanket folded into a tidy square. Then she remembers *why* Inés is screeching. "Wait a moment," she says to Leonor. "I'll go with you."

For now, Inés is the only one howling at the base of Mount Linda Vista. But not for long. Soon the dawn chorus of birds will give way to the hollering

14

of furious princesas whose gowns have been torn to shreds. Dominga doesn't want to miss a thing.

Outside, princesas, still in their nightdresses, stumble out of their tents and follow the sound of Inés's yelling.

Dominga finds Dalia and lets Leonor go on ahead. "It sounds as if our plan is working," she whispers when Leonor is too far away to hear.

"She's loud enough to wake the villains at the B.A.D.," Dalia agrees. She clutches the locket around her neck. Inside—as Dominga and hardly anyone else knows—is a portrait of Dalia's mother. Dalia's mother, who happens to be the head villain of the B.A.D., and who Dalia is even more desperate to impress than Dominga is.

Profesora Colibrí stands outside the wardrobe tent with one arm around Inés. In her free hand, she flutters her fan.

"¿Qué pasó?" Princesa Eloísa, Dalia's suite mate in Casita Emerald, asks. She straightens her tiara, made of five gold bands and a sprinkle of emeralds that look like musical notes.

Inés wriggles out from under Profesora Colibrí's arm. She looks back at the princesas gathered around her, eyes flickering as if she's counting to be sure everyone is present. She pulls a silk handkerchief out of her sleeve and waves it in the air like a wilted lily. Then she dabs her nose with it. She steps forward.

Dominga loops her arm through Dalia's and swallows back an eager squeal as the princesas quiet down.

"I'll tell you what happened," Inés begins. "I woke up early." She looks up at Profesora Colibrí. "I wanted to be perfectly punctual for our hike, you know." The profesora nods, and Inés looks toward the crowd again. "But when I put on my hiking gown—which has crushed opals woven into the fabric, by the way—I found *this*."

She whips her cloak back over her shoulders and reveals the gown.

"It's even worse in the daylight," Dominga mutters, grimacing at the golden threads hanging from the ragged edge of what's left of Inés's dress.

Dalia grins. "I know."

Profesora Colibrí's mouth drops open, and she covers it with her fan.

"Perhaps it was a badger," Princesa Carmen suggests. "Dalia says they're very good at tearing through dirt."

Dominga turns to Dalia, who shrugs. "I didn't think anyone was listening," she whispers.

"Or maybe you didn't pack quite carefully enough," Princesa Lizeth says. "You *were* in a terrible hurry to get to the campsite and have first pick of the cots."

Inés's cheeks turn bright pink. Nearly as pink as the clouds on the horizon as the sun continues to rise. She throws down her handkerchief, and Dominga watches it flutter to the dirt.

"It was not a badger!" Inés shouts with a stomp of her foot that sends a cloud of dust over her ankles. She huffs as she swats it away. "And I most certainly know how to pack, thank you very much, *Lizeth*."

Dominga tilts her head toward Dalia and covers her mouth with her hand. "She said 'thank you,' but I don't think she really means it."

Dalia shakes her head. "She didn't even curtsy," she murmurs back.

Inés lifts her chin. "This was no accident, and I'm not the only victim!"

She pulls back the flap of the wardrobe tent. The gowns hang from the rack, exactly the way Dalia and Dominga left them. Only they're not quite gowns anymore. More like half gowns, with a tangle of fabric scraps beneath them like a rainbow that's been minced to pieces by Chef Luís-Esteban.

"They're all ruined!" Leonor cries, pushing toward the garment rack. She pulls her gown—pale blue with small white silk moths hand-painted across the bodice—from its hanger. She holds it against her chest. Once, it would have fluttered at her ankles. Now it falls to just below her knees.

"Not *all* ruined," Inés corrects her, looking not quite so heartbroken now. "Exactly two of the gowns are perfectly fine." She pauses. "Not that you could *really* call them perfect. Not that you would even call them gowns. But anyway, any guesses who they belong to?"

Dominga squeezes Dalia's arm. Dalia squeezes back. Here it comes. The moment they will be seen for the villains they truly are. Dominga looks up, hopeful one of the ravens from the B.A.D. is circling the sky, watching them.

"You know," says Carmen, stepping out from behind the wild salmonberry bush where she went to change, "this isn't so bad." She looks down at her gown, mint-and-pistachio-striped and half as long as it used to be. "It'll be easier to keep cool in this. And I won't have to worry about dragging it through the mud."

"Or getting caught in my wheels," Leonor agrees, holding her dress out in front of her as her shock turns into curiosity.

Valentina begins gathering up the fabric scraps.

"I can braid these into ropes in case we need to do any climbing along the way."

"Or we can use them as bandages," Jacinta says, "if we run into any hurt animals."

Inés's face is pinker than the sky now. Pinker even than the salmonberries.

"It was Dalia and Dominga!" She is screeching again. "They did it! They destroyed our dresses!" But no one pays her much attention. They are all too busy trying on their new gowns.

Profesora Colibrí sets a hand on Dominga's shoulder and another on Dalia's. "Bravo," she says. "A true princesa is always innovative. She challenges us to see things in a new way. Your designs will help us have a much more pleasant hike."

Dalia hangs her head. Her curls fall over her eyes. Dominga glances at the sky, where the ravens from the B.A.D. circle farther and farther away. "Gracias, Profesora," she mumbles with a slow, tired curtsy.

Valentina taps her shoulder when she rises. She offers Dominga her scissors. "You must have forgotten to do yours."

This isn't what they planned. It almost never is. But the princesas have a point. Her gown would be far more practical if it was just a bit shorter. And think how annoyed Mamá would be if she knew Dominga had ripped it apart.

She takes the scissors. She finds her smoky-gray gown on the rack. She is about to cut into the skirt when Dalia scowls.

"*Dominga!* What are you doing?"

Right. This is a disaster, after all.

Another screech tears through the morning. They turn their heads toward Inés, who is hopping on one foot, waving her hands. "It *licked* me!"

Don Ignacio comes scuttling back to Dalia and dives over the top of her boot.

Perhaps not a complete disaster.

CHAPTER 3

Dalia and Dominga fall to the end of the line of princesas making their way up the mountain trail.

"I'll write to my tailors as soon as we get back to the palace." Inés's voice drifts down from the front of the line. "I'll have all my gowns shortened. They won't be at all surprised to hear that I've started yet another trend."

Dominga does not hear Lizeth's reply, but sees

her quicken her pace to get ahead of Inés.

After a while, Eloísa begins to strum the small guitar she carries strapped to her back. The princesas start to sing. Dalia stops. She turns her face to the sky and yells. An eagle squawks back at her from its nest.

"Don't worry," Dominga says, pulling Dalia along. "There's still time. We'll think up something even ghastlier before this hike is over, I'm sure of it."

From the pocket of her gown—which she tries not to wish were a little shorter, a little lighter—Dominga pulls out a book with a worn cloth cover. It is a diary that Princesa Paloma (or Princesa *Perfecta*, as Dominga usually refers to her older sister) gave her. Paloma graduated the year before, but Dominga still can't seem to escape her. As Fairest of the F.A.I.R., Perfecta's portrait will hang forever in the palace gallery.

But Paloma can't stop Dominga from using the diary as a spell book, a place to record wicked plots and evil schemes. Though, lately, Dominga has been filling it mostly with recipes.

She flips through the pages. "There must be something in here we haven't tried. Oh!" She stops on a page. "A swarm of wasps to chase them down the hill!" Next to the idea, she's sketched a rock knocking a wasp's nest off a tree branch as its angry inhabitants buzz outside.

"We've already tried fire ants," Dalia says. She twists her curls into a bun, then picks a stick up off the ground to hold it in place. "And robins," she adds. "Not to mention rats."

"Hmm." Dominga cannot argue. They have not had much success with animal schemes.

The temperature, once warm, is inching

toward hot. Dominga's glasses slide down her sweaty nose. She pushes them back up and lifts her eyes off the page to study the royally neat line of princesas ahead of them.

"Not *actual* animals, then," she says, a new idea taking shape in her mind. Her voice rises as the details become clearer. "Monsters. Like the ones in the stories they were all telling last night. We convince them they're real." She sketches the two of them, screaming through the forest like the owl-witch from Jacinta's tale. "They'll be too frightened to ever leave the castle again—*if* they even make it back, that is." They might be so terrified, they scatter off in all directions, lost for eternity, while Dalia and Dominga escape to the B.A.D.

Dalia catches a dragonfly in her hands, watches its glassy wings quiver for a moment, then sets it free. "They'd probably want to invite the monster back to the palace for dinner," she says.

It's true. The princesas are more courteous and more courageous than Dalia and Dominga first expected. In fact, it's one of the first Rules for Villains that Dominga wrote in her spell book: *Never underestimate a princesa.*

"We should wait," Dalia says finally. "We will seize our chance when it comes. Villains must be patient."

Dominga nods. *Villains must be patient.* She adds the new rule to her spell book, then shuts it.

Silently, they follow the princesas to the top of Mount Linda Vista.

When they reach the summit, Princesa Floramaria is waiting with a mini bouquet of wildflowers she picked along the way. Purple lupines and fiery poppies and cheery daisies. "We've made it!"

With a strained, shaky smile, Dalia steps sideways toward a nearby circle of crows. She reaches into her pocket and pulls out a crust of bread, left over from breakfast. She breaks off pieces and tosses them to the cawing birds. Dominga baked the bread herself. It's one of her newest recipes, made with rosemary picked fresh from the palace garden. A small, stinging part of her would have preferred to see Dalia gobble up the bread herself. But at least it hasn't gone to waste.

A brown fedora with a blue-green feather tucked into the band sits just off-center on Profesora Colibrí's head. She stands at the edge of a lookout, fluttering her fan to beckon the princesas.

"Don't dawdle!" she warbles to Dalia and Dominga, who still lag behind. Dalia throws her last bit of bread to the crows before she and Dominga gather alongside the others.

Profesora Colibrí turns and opens her arms wide. "Observe!" she sings.

The princesas gaze out at the view from the top of Mount Linda Vista. Eloísa stops strumming her guitar strings. Floramaria lets the last of her flowers fall. Even Inés is quiet. All they can hear is the rustle of leaves and the faint chirping of finches.

"I can see the palace from here," Leonor says after a while, her voice so soft the gentle breeze could carry it away.

Dominga finds the clock tower, the sunken garden. The woods and the golden gates that closed behind her when she first arrived at the

F.A.I.R. She can almost make out a wisp of smoke from the kitchens where Chef Luís-Esteban will have started preparing dinner by now. It seems smaller from here than it does when she's stuck in the middle of it.

She glances at Dalia, wondering if she thinks so too. But Dalia has bent down to lift Don Ignacio out of her boot so that he can sneak a glimpse of the palace grounds.

"Now look beyond," Profesora Colibrí says.

Past the gates is a village of thatch-roofed cottages with orange and pink bougainvilleas climbing their white walls. A cobblestone path wanders playfully through them, then races out toward the surrounding fields. From up here the fields look like a patchwork quilt of green and yellow squares, dotted here and there with goats and cows.

"Princesas must become part of their communities," Profesora Colibrí says.

But how can they be a part of the community when they are stuck inside the palace?

As if in answer to Dominga's silent question, Profesora Colibrí continues.

"To introduce yourselves to our neighbors and spread the spirit of welcome, all first-year princesas must throw a ball."

The princesas gasp.

"With dancing?" Princesa Pilar asks.

"And music?" says Eloísa.

Profesora Colibrí closes her fan and tucks it into the sash at her waist. "It is all up to you, princesas."

Dalia leans her head toward Dominga's. "Did you hear that? It's all up to us." Her black eyes gleam.

CHAPTER 4

Inés tosses her curls over her shoulder. "I knew all about the Ball de la Bienvenida," she says. "My dressmakers have been working on my gown for months."

Princesa Marisol raises a hand. Her tiara is made of golden rays, as thin as needles. "I can help anyone who still needs a gown," she offers. "I do all my own sewing."

Profesora Colibrí clears her throat. "An

enchanting ball takes much more than lovely gowns."

The princesas must organize themselves into committees to plan everything from the decorations to the music to the menu to the invitations. And they will not be working solely with princesas from their own Casitas.

"Choose the committee where your talents can bloom," Profesora Colibrí says. "And remember that each of you shares responsibility for the evening's success. The princesa who contributes the most to the ball—as voted on by all her classmates—will earn fifty gems for her Casita's chalice."

Hushed murmurs ripple over the crowd of princesas. With fifty more gems, the winning princesa and her Casita will be almost certain to earn the freedom to explore the village below.

Dominga removes her glasses and cleans them

with the ruffle at her wrist. She smooths out the wrinkles in her skirt as if she is about to step down a golden staircase and into a ballroom for the first time.

Paloma used to write about the balls in her long letters home. Those were the only parts of her letters that Dominga ever paid attention to. The only parts that didn't leave her drowsy with boredom.

Paloma wrote about gowns that swished like flowers in a spring breeze. About music that burbled over the dance floor. About new faces from the village with new stories to tell. But best of all, Paloma wrote about the food. Course after course. Roasted peppers stuffed with goat cheese. Rich, velvety mole with a list of ingredients so long it would fill five entire pages in Dominga's spell book. Desserts made of chocolate spiced with cinnamon and anise and a pinch of chili. Sugar spun into golden clouds.

And for the first time, Dominga will see it all for herself. She stands on her toes and raises a hand. "I volunteer to work on the menu!" she shouts without thinking.

"Bravo, Princesa." Profesora Colibrí applauds. "It seems that, like your sister, you are well on your way to becoming Fairest of the F.A.I.R."

Inés pushes her way forward. "*I'm* in charge of decorations," she announces. "I'll make sure the palace looks perfect for our guests."

Dominga shrinks down. Her cheeks go warm. The last thing she wants to be is Fairest of the F.A.I.R. Obviously. At least she hopes it's obvious. All she wants is the chance to show off the techniques she's been learning alongside Chef

Luís-Esteban. To try out even more daring recipes. Pastries filled with rainbow-colored cream
that turn everything you say into a song for
exactly three minutes. Pies that breathe out glit-
tery steam—and a whisper of good luck—when
you cut into them.

Still, she can't bear to look at Dalia.

And then she notices Dalia is no longer beside
her. She has drifted away from the huddle of
princesas and collapsed into a swamp-green
heap, leaning against a tree trunk. Don Ignacio
rests in her hand, and she gently strokes his head
with her fingernail. She doesn't look up when
Dominga approaches, even though she must have
heard her footsteps.

Dominga remembers a story Dalia once told
her. That when she was younger, before she came

to the F.A.I.R., she went to live with her abuelos on their farm. Her grandmother and grandfather had tried to throw Dalia a welcome party. Only, when their neighbors realized Dalia's mother was a notorious villain, none of them came.

There are many reasons the thought of a ball might make Dalia want to run away, Dominga realizes. This is probably one of them. But maybe Dominga can convince her that it might not be so awful. That, for once, they might have fun at the F.A.I.R. Before they escape to the B.A.D. for good, that is.

"Are you thinking about the party?" she asks, sitting down next to Dalia. "The one at the farm?"

Dalia guides Don Ignacio back into her boot. She blows her curls out of her face and looks up. She narrows her eyes at Dominga.

"Why did you volunteer to help with the ball?

This was the chance we've been waiting for. To *ruin* it."

Ruin it?

Of course.

Ruining the ball would be the perfect way to show the B.A.D. just how dreadful they are. The night could be a spectacular failure, and all because of them. She should have thought of that. Why didn't she?

And yet, she thinks, perhaps just this once they can take a break. Even villains go to balls, after all. Often as uninvited guests, but still. Dalia said herself that they needed to be patient. A night of music and dancing and desserts might be just what they need to sharpen their thinking, refresh their imaginations, and dream up their most gruesome plan yet.

"Well . . . It's that . . ." Dominga starts and stops

and starts again, unsure how to explain it. "What I was thinking was—"

Dalia interrupts her. "I had already come up with five different ways we could sabotage it. I thought you'd have some ideas too."

Then Dalia freezes. She stands, and sunlight hits her face as though an idea has just struck her.

"Wait a moment," she says.

"Of course," Dominga agrees. At least she doesn't have to speak now.

"I was wrong," Dalia says.

Dominga's shoulders relax. "Thank you. I knew you'd—"

Dalia isn't finished. "That's exactly what you were doing, wasn't it?"

"Huh?" Dominga scrunches her nose.

"I can't believe I didn't realize it." Dalia pulls Dominga up by her wrists. "You volunteered for the menu committee so that you could spoil the food! Make the princesas sick! Turn their teeth black! Give them never-ending hiccups! The possibilities are endless!"

Dominga's eyes dart away from Dalia's. "Yes," she says, laughing nervously. "That is exactly what I had in mind."

Princesa Leonor comes toward them. "What are you doing over here?" she asks. "Come back. We're nearly finished choosing committees."

CHAPTER 5

Dalia and Dominga follow Leonor and rejoin the rest of their class. Profesora Colibrí sits perched on a boulder, fluttering her fan. Above her head, in a cloud of lilac mist, a pen floats, writing down all the committee assignments as the princesas call them out.

"I've joined decorations," Leonor says, pointing to her name, which glows silver in the air above the profesora. "I'm not exactly looking forward to working with Inés, but I already have so many ideas. We could paint some giant murals to hang from the rafters. Or create a mosaic labyrinth on the floor out of smashed bits of the palace dinnerware. You can join us, Dalia. We'll need lots of help."

The color drains from Dalia's face. She stares, blinking at Leonor as if hopelessly lost.

"Maybe music," Dominga suggests, steering Dalia toward another group.

Leonor pushes toward the team of princesas who are arguing over the ball's theme. "Wait!" she says. "I've already told you, it *can't* be Enchanted Castle. We wouldn't need any decorations at all!"

Dominga spots Eloísa sitting cross-legged with her guitar in a patch of grass. "Think of all the haunting melodies you can plan," Dominga tells Dalia, walking toward Eloísa. "You can sneak in

an enchantment that keeps the princesas dancing until they wear through the soles of their
slippers." Didn't they hear about such a spell in
a fairy tale? "Or one that hypnotizes them into
dancing like chickens."

Dalia lifts her head. Her eyes sparkle. "Or spiders. The dance of the peacock spider is truly
terrifying."

But when they get to the music committee,
they find that Eloísa is teaching the rest of the
committee a song of her own.

"Sit," she says, patting the ground beside her.
"We'll make room for you."

The princesas widen their circle.

"We're composing a welcome song for our
guests," Eloísa continues. She strums her guitar,
and the chords are so monstrously melodic that
Dominga shudders.

"I . . . don't think I'm right for the music committee," Dalia says, backing away. "I can't play a note, and I sing like a bullfrog."

Dominga happens to think bullfrogs have a lovely song. But she knows Dalia is simply making excuses, so she doesn't argue.

Instead, they walk toward the last committee, in charge of the dancing. Pilar is leading the group in a waltz, clapping to keep their steps in time.

"Oh, good, I was hoping you'd join us," Pilar says when she notices Dalia and Dominga watching. She leaps over to them. "I want to choreograph a dance with woodland creatures. Box-stepping fawns, promenading rabbits. You can teach them, can't you? Marisol says she'll make us matching tutus. For the animals too!"

As hard as she tries, Dominga cannot picture

Dalia joining this committee. Or wearing a tutu.

"I suppose . . ." Dominga begins, not really wanting to say it. "There's always . . ." She forces herself. "Menu?"

It's not that she doesn't want to have Dalia on her committee. Dalia is her friend. The first person to see her for who she truly is. It's just that, if Dalia is on the committee, Dominga won't be able to prepare any of the recipes she's been dreaming up. She feels slightly sick for even thinking it.

"Dominga!" Jacinta calls from the ancient tree stump the menu committee is sitting around. "We're all here, and we're ready to get started."

Dominga looks up at Dalia and gulps. "Well?" she asks.

Dalia shakes her head. Her curls fall into her eyes again. "No, we should split up," she replies. "We can do more damage that way."

Dominga hopes her relief doesn't show on her face. "It's too bad," she says. "But you're right, of course."

Together, they gaze out across the mountaintop. The teams are already buzzing with excitement. "So, which will you choose?"

Profesora Colibrí strides toward them, the pen still floating over her head.

"We better hide, or the profesora is going to decide for you," Dominga chatters in squirrel-speak.

"Behind that pile of pine cones," Dalia chirps back.

They are too late. "Princesa Dalia," Profesora Colibrí trills. "You are the only princesa who has not yet selected a committee."

Inés comes scampering behind her. "She doesn't want to help, Profesora," she says. "Dalia doesn't like balls. It's almost as if she doesn't really *belong* here."

Dalia straightens. "Of course I want to help," she says, smiling up at Profesora Colibrí. "I want to be *awfully* helpful," she adds under her breath in squirrel-speak.

Dominga presses her lips together to keep from giggling.

"Bueno," Profesora Colibrí says, staring down her long, thin nose at Dalia. Her vest glistens silver and red in the sun. "I have the perfect role for you."

She takes Dalia's hand and leads her to the center of the summit. "Atención, princesas," she says, clapping her fan against her palm. She positions Dalia in front of her and rests her hands on top of Dalia's shoulders. To Dominga, it looks almost as if she's trying to keep Dalia from escaping.

And the horrified look on Dalia's face tells Dominga that's exactly what she has in mind.

Whatever this is, you have to get me out of it, Dalia's eyes seem to plead.

Dominga frowns in reply. *I'm sorry, but I don't see how.*

"Each of you has chosen an important role," Profesora Colibrí says. "But there is one role left, and it seems it will go to Princesa Dalia. I hereby declare her la Reina de la Fiesta. She will ensure that the plans you are forming separately—the decorations, the music, the menu, the dancing—all come together in a harmonious ball. And, even more importantly, she will send out the invitations on our behalf."

The magical pen glides through the air.

La Reina de la Fiesta, it writes in silvery ink. And next to that, *Princesa Dalia.*

Profesora Colibrí opens her fan, and all the names fall into it. The pen disappears in a puff of smoke, and a sash appears in its place. It drifts slowly down and settles across Dalia's chest, the satin pink glowing bright against her swampy gown.

The princesas applaud. Even Dominga. What else can she do?

"*Excuse me?*" Dalia and Inés say at the same time.

Profesora Colibrí ignores them. "Now, gather your belongings, princesas, and be sure to drink some water. We must hike back down before we lose the light. Quickly, please."

She begins walking toward the trail, and the princesas scramble to catch up. Dalia doesn't move. She stares down at the sash. *La Reina de la Fiesta*, it says in sparkling script. Very official.

Inés takes one look at it, scowls, then races after Profesora Colibrí.

"But, Profesora," she protests, "I didn't know there was such a thing as Queen of the Ball. Don't you think it should go to someone else? Someone a little more like a princesa?"

Profesora Colibrí doesn't stop walking. "Everyone here is a princesa, Inés. Whom would you suggest?"

"Well . . . me!"

The profesora smiles. "You have already volunteered for the decorations committee."

"But Dalia needs my help," Inés insists. "Just look at her." Inés points back to Dalia, still frozen.

Dominga nudges her. "Dalia," she whispers. "Say something."

Profesora Colibrí turns and studies Dalia. "Hmmm." She taps her fan against her lips. "I suppose you might be right, Princesa Inés." She flicks her fan and begins walking again. "Bueno, you are co-reinas."

Another pink sash appears, this time across Inés's chest.

Dalia finally unfreezes, but it's only to squeeze her eyes shut and groan.

CHAPTER 6

A *catastrophe*. Dalia has repeated the word so many times that it has begun to sound like nonsense. Dominga worries that Profesora Colibrí's magic has somehow left her incapable of saying anything else.

Although Dalia has a point. The thought of partnering with Inés makes Dominga shudder. Still, she tries to help Dalia feel better. "It might not be as bad as you think?"

Dalia, who has been muttering to herself, her hands balled into tight fists as she stomps along the mountain trail, suddenly stops. She turns to Dominga and swipes her curls out of her face.

"Not as bad as I think?" she demands.

Dominga cringes, but at least Dalia is saying something different.

"Not as bad as I think?" Dalia says again, so loudly this time that Profesora Colibrí, at the head of the line, glances back.

How unusually reckless of Dalia. She is typically so careful and cunning.

"Is everything all right, princesas?" Profesora Colibrí calls, hands cupped around her mouth.

"Everything is fine, profesora," Dominga calls back with a quick curtsy. "We're just *awfully* excited about the ball."

Profesora Colibrí nods and continues walking. "I am not surprised," she sings. "It is the highlight of every princesa's first year at the F.A.I.R."

Dominga doubts it will be the highlight of Dalia's. Though she wishes somehow it could be.

Dalia seems to have recovered. She lifts up her long green skirts to hop over a squirrel hole and comes down in a puddle. Mud splashes up at both of them, but it doesn't break Dalia's stride. She lowers her voice. "Inés is the only person, besides you, who knows who my mother is," she says. "She must be plotting something."

Dominga adjusts her tiara, silver with clusters of round opals like bubbles in a potion bottle. It can be a bit poke-y. "*Do* princesas plot?"

"Maybe not," Dalia says. "But I'm still going to be stuck working with her for four whole weeks."

Dominga picks out Inés's amber gown in the line of princesas ahead of them. Already, she is darting up and down, insisting that the princesas tell her what they have planned so far and assigning them impossible deadlines.

"By tomorrow," she is shouting to Leonor, "I want to see a full presentation of your five best theme ideas. *Including* full color schemes and sketches of the decor and layout. And if I were you, I'd prepare six just to be safe."

Leonor steers her chair away from her.

Working with Inés is not even the worst of it, Dominga knows. Dalia will have to explain to the B.A.D. why she was in charge of a ball. For *princesas.*

"They're never going to let me in after this," Dalia complains, kicking at a small gray pebble. It bounces off ahead of her. "La Reina de la Fiesta? Can you imagine what they'll say? I don't think there's anyone in the history of the B.A.D. who has ever worn a pink sash!"

She stares down at the sash and tugs at it, but it remains stubbornly snug across her shoulder. When she lets it go, the sash ripples. The snags and wrinkles her fingers left behind smooth themselves out.

Dalia is right. A true villain wouldn't be caught composing a sunny welcome song. Or arranging tiny tiles into a labyrinth mosaic—unless it was the kind of labyrinth that led straight to a dragon's smoldering den.

The infamous Ball for the Banished, held annually at the B.A.D., is known for its poison-flavored candy apples, glowing yellow green.

Its haunting melodies plucked by ghostly hands on harp strings and plinked by skeleton fingers on piano keys. Its decorations that send some guests screaming from the entrance in terror. Dominga spins. Her dress twirls out around her ankles as she pictures herself at the center of it all. Then she trips on a maple root.

"Are you quite all right?" Dalia asks.

Dominga can't tell whether she's asking about the fall or the spin. "Oh yes," she answers, brushing dirt off her palms. "I was only thinking that . . ." She stops herself. There's no way the ball the princesas plan will be anything like the B.A.D.'s.

"Yes?" Dalia asks.

But then again, why shouldn't it be? A new scheme simmers in Dominga's mind like a fresh batch of potion, pungent and powerful.

"You said you wanted to ruin the ball, didn't you?" Dominga asks, gazing back at the mist-cloaked towers of the B.A.D., not so far away as they once seemed.

"Exactly," Dalia answers. "Ruin the ball. Spoil the ball. Not *organize* the ball."

Dominga spins again, this time to face her. "But don't you see?" she asks, her voice rising as the solution becomes clear. She is surprised that Dalia, a true villain from the very start, didn't think of it first. Well, if she's being terribly honest, she is not *only* surprised. She is proud of herself.

"Don't you *see*?" she yells, taking hold of Dalia's shoulders and shaking them.

Eloísa, marching a few paces ahead, turns around. "See what?"

Drat. Dominga lets go of Dalia's shoulders. She really must learn to be more secretive, more sly.

There's so much about villainy she still needs to practice, and there is no better (or, rather, worse) place than the B.A.D.

"See . . . the . . . wild strawberries," Dominga says, gesturing toward the ground. "They should ripen just in time for the ball."

Eloísa's eyes drift to the berries growing along the edge of the path, pink and green beneath blossoms like white bonnets. "They do look delicious," she says. "I think I'll write a song about them." She pulls her guitar around and starts strumming.

Dominga can hardly stand another song, but at least the noise will make it harder for anyone else to hear what she is about to tell Dalia.

"You were saying?" Dalia whispers.

"Don't you see?" Dominga begins again. "That as Reina de la Fiesta, you will have a better chance than anyone to sabotage the ball. You will be in charge of everything. You can scramble the arrangements. You can turn the teams against one another. You can organize a party fit for the worst villains."

It couldn't be more horrible if they'd planned it this way from the beginning. "You can turn the ball into a complete disaster. In front of the whole village! And I'll help. The B.A.D. will think we're desperately cunning to have plotted it all."

Dominga studies Dalia's face as they begin walking again. She can see that, behind her eyes, Dalia is calculating. Sizing up the challenge. She is interested, but she is not yet convinced.

"Without Inés, perhaps," Dalia says, twirling a curl around her finger. "Working in secret. But Inés will be looking out for anything unusual."

Inés will want this ball to be flawless. More elegant than any other ball the palace has ever seen.

"But we are true villains," Dominga insists. "We can outwit even the most persistent princesa. We'll prove it."

Dalia's eyes flit to Inés, whose curls bounce beneath her golden tiara, glinting in the sun. "It would be nice to defeat her."

"Wickedly nice," Dominga agrees.

And with Dalia in charge of all the tricks, what's the harm if Dominga cooks up some delicious treats instead of disgusting ones?

CHAPTER 7

After breakfast the next morning, Dominga retreats to Casita Opal. Inside the study are armchairs as soft as feather pillows and cushions that shimmer pink and purple and gold depending on how the light hits them. She pulls off her boots and digs her toes into the pearly plush carpet.

Sun pours in through stained glass windows the colors of mint and strawberry ice cream. Someone has left one of the windows open a crack, and a breeze fills the room with the smell of the jasmine growing on the trellis outside.

The rest of the Opal princesas have rushed away to all corners of the palace to work on their preparations for the ball. That means the suite is empty. Quiet. Exactly what Dominga needs to make some plans of her own. She reaches under the chair for the stack of ancient cookbooks, borrowed from Chef Luís-Esteban, that she has hidden there. The one on top is a book of desserts. She brings it to her lap, settles into the chair, and opens it.

She is running her finger down the table of contents, deciding whether to start with cakes or tarts or custards, when a tap at the window startles her.

She straightens her glasses and slides farther down into the chair. It's probably that black-and-white-speckled chicken she met by accident during her first week at the F.A.I.R. The bird hasn't stopped following her around ever since. She is noisy and needy, and Dominga would rather not entertain her in these precious moments of solitude. If Dominga is very still, perhaps the hen will think there is no one inside and go away.

The tapping stops.

"Bueno," Dominga says to herself, promising to pay a visit to the chicken coop later that afternoon. "I'll start with tarts." She turns to the page with a recipe for a dark chocolate tart with sugar-glazed walnuts and rose-petal cream.

There is another knock at the window.

This time a harsh hiss follows it. "Are you in there?" a voice asks in turkey vulture. "Open up."

Dalia. Dominga jumps to her feet, slams the

recipe book shut, and shoves it back under the chair. "One moment!" Dalia will find out about her dinner plans sooner or later. But Dominga would prefer that it happen in the middle of a ball that is crumbling into chaos. In other words, when Dalia is least likely to notice. Or mind.

Dominga takes her spell book from her pocket and goes to the window. Dalia has climbed the trellis and is waiting just outside.

"What are you doing in there?" Dalia asks, looking up.

"Just thinking about food for the ball," Dominga says, tapping on the spell book and avoiding Dalia's eyes. "The menu committee is meeting later, and I want to have some ideas."

Dalia grins. "Dreadful ideas, I imagine."

Dominga pulls a pencil from her bun and gnaws on the end of it without answering.

Fortunately, Dalia changes the subject. "I'm going to visit the decorations committee," she says, holding on to the trellis with one hand and pointing with the other. "Do you want to come with me? You can help give them some terrible ideas."

On the one hand, this will interfere with her research. On the other hand, she needs to be sure the ball is a massive enough mess that the villains of the B.A.D. overlook her recipes fit for royalty. "Let's go," Dominga says, and clambers out the window.

They find the committee in the art studio. Leonor is drawing on a piece of brown paper that stretches across a long tabletop. The other princesas on the committee huddle around her.

"You're here!" Leonor says, noticing Dalia and Dominga. "Finally. We have a theme to show you." She waves them over. Wooden chairs scrape across the floor as the princesas shift to open their circle.

Leonor picks up one of the many brushes scattered across the table and dips it into a pot of orange paint. When she lifts it, a few drops spatter to the floor. They melt into the tiles and become part of a swirling rainbow made of all the paint that has ever been spilled there.

Leonor sweeps the brush across the paper, and Dalia and Dominga peer down at her work. Dominga recognizes the palace's Great Hall and the four chalices that hold each Casita's gems. But instead of the delicate banners that usually flutter from the rafters, Leonor has painted orange spirals of sparks and flame.

"The Phoenix Feast!" Leonor announces.

"We'll arrange a bouquet of golden feathers at every table," Floramaria says.

"And make lanterns out of glowing embers," adds Valentina.

"And I'll paint fireworks on the windows," Leonor says. "With Maestro Pinto's enchanted paints, it will look like they're really exploding."

Dominga can already imagine dishes that will bring the theme even more vividly to life. Burnt caramel custard and seared peaches with vanilla honey. She reaches for her spell book, wanting to write it all down.

But not yet.

Not with Dalia right here.

"Well?" Valentina asks, bouncing in her chair. "What do you think?"

The princesas stare at Dalia, hungry for her reaction.

"Fire is good," she says at last. "Flames sound promising. But . . ."

Leonor leans in closer. "But?"

"Well, if you're thinking of mythical creatures, why not a dragon's lair instead?" Dalia suggests. "That's even more exciting."

"She's right!" Dominga agrees, stepping forward. "You could turn the fireplace into its den, complete with sour dragon's breath. And fill the corners of the hall with piles of ash and coats of armor that have burnt to a crisp."

"That would be *unique*," Valentina says, coughing as though she is already choking on the smoky air. "Not very festive, though."

Dalia isn't finished. She leans over the table and sweeps away three half-filled pots of paint with one wave of her arm. The floor tiles drink up the spilled colors. "Or how about Nahuelito's cave?"

Floramaria's nose wrinkles. "The lake monster?"

Even better, Dominga thinks. *I'll bake fish pies.*

Leonor is quiet. She taps her paintbrush against her temple. "I'm not so sure about dragon breath," she says after a while. "But I like the idea of even more magical creatures. We can call it the Mythical Masquerade!"

Footsteps thunder down the hall. "Don't be ridiculous!"

Leonor sighs and sets down the paintbrush. "You're not on the decorations committee, Inés!" she calls out. "Remember?" Her eyes roll up toward the ceiling.

Inés steps into the studio. The crystals in her tiara sparkle. She pulls her cream-colored gloves over her elbows.

"But, as Reina de la Fiesta, I must approve every decision," she says. "*Remember?*" She points to her sash.

"Co-reina," Dominga corrects her. "Dalia has a

say too, and the theme is settled. It's too bad you arrived so late."

Inés waves her fingers as if Dominga is a pesky fruit fly hovering around a peach she has her eye on.

"We agreed that since you didn't like Enchanted Castle for some reason, the theme would be Wildflower Wonderland," Inés tells Leonor. "I thought it was a perfectly generous compromise." She saunters to the art table, picks up the paintbrush Leonor set down, and dips it in a splotch of pink paint from Valentina's palette. With a few quick strokes, she paints a flower.

"Wildflower Wonderland will be a celebration of the natural beauty of the palace grounds," she continues, lifting an arm and gesturing toward the gardens outside. "Besides, my dressmaker is already working on my gown."

"So we've heard," Leonor mutters, pulling another, finer brush out of the front pocket of her smock. She paints a fairy, with ferocious teeth and flashing eyes, clutching Inés's flower.

The fairy looks like it flew straight out of a nightmare. *Impressive*, Dominga thinks. *Wicked, even.*

"*You* agreed to Wildflower Wonderland," Leonor says. "Not us."

"It's not that we don't like it," Floramaria adds. "I adore flowers."

"But we were hoping to try something a little surprising," Valentina says.

Dalia pulls a charcoal pencil from a jar at the end of the table. "Precisely." She draws a small black spider next to the fairy. "Something that's *never* been seen at the palace before."

Dominga can hardly conceal her cackle.

Inés's jaw tenses, and her cheeks bloom

cherry-blossom pink. But she keeps her voice light and airy. "The whole point of a ball is to be predictable," she sings, waltzing to the center of the room. She notices the paint-spattered floor for the first time and frowns. "We tell our guests when to arrive and when to leave, what they will be eating, and what to wear." She stops twirling and turns to the table, hands on her hips. "They want to know what to expect!"

Dominga covers her mouth with her hand and squeaks in rat-speak, "I'm going to sneak away before she starts asking questions about the menu."

"Terrible idea," Dalia squeaks back. By which, Dominga knows, she means it is a very good one.

CHAPTER
8

What Profesora Colibrí could have been thinking to put someone like Dalia in charge of the ball, Inés will never understand. So she doesn't even bother trying. It's clear that Dalia doesn't know the first thing about balls. Considering who her mother is, can it be any surprise?

Instead of arguing, Dalia should be *thanking* Inés for keeping her secret. Her dark secret. The secret that Inés is bursting to tell: that the portrait Dalia keeps hidden inside her locket is of her mother. And that Dalia's mother just happens to be the notorious director of the B.A.D., Profesora de la Sombra.

But, of course, that would mean Inés would have to explain *how* she knows who the director of the B.A.D. is in the first place. She shudders. "Never," she says aloud without meaning to.

Leonor tilts her head and squints. The same look she gives her canvas when she's puzzling out a new painting. The real puzzle is why it's taking her so long to ask whether Inés would sit for a portrait.

"What do you mean, 'never'?" Leonor asks. "That we've never had a mythical-creature-themed ball before? Or that you'd never agree to it?"

Inés crosses her arms over her chest, tilts up her chin, and flutters her eyelashes. "Both," she says. "It's all wrong. Just ask Dominga. Her older sister was Fairest of the . . . Huh?"

Inés turns and realizes Dominga is no longer in the art studio. Dominga is forever disappearing, never around when Inés most needs her. The two of them could have teamed up to become the most perfect princesas ever to have graced these halls. Inés would have been the *most* most perfect. Naturally. Still, she would have made sure Dominga felt as if it had been a close call. But ever since the very first day, when Inés went out of her way to be so *awfully* friendly, Dominga has seemed as though she isn't the slightest bit interested in being named Fairest of the F.A.I.R.

It's probably an act, Inés has decided. To convince Profesora Colibrí of how humble she is.

But where's the sense in that? Inés isn't afraid to let anyone know what she wants. And what she wants is to be Fairest of the F.A.I.R. She has been preparing her entire life. For as long as she can remember, her parents have praised her effortless style. Her brilliant wit. Her impeccable charm. She is the *best*.

And if she isn't the best, then what is she?

The question isn't worth answering. It isn't even the point. The point is that every tiny detail makes a difference, and she is not about to let these clueless princesas ruin things with creativity and silly surprises.

"Um, Inés?" Dalia is tapping her shoulder. She's wearing another one of those dismal gowns the color of a dirt road after a thunderstorm. She seems to have an endless supply of them. "You were saying?"

Inés takes a slow, steadying breath. She remembers the golden tiara atop her head, expertly secured with pearl-tipped hairpins. She straightens her shoulders. "Never mind," she says. "Dominga would agree with me, I'm quite sure of it. Now, we've wasted enough time. The theme of the ball is Wildflower Wonderland and that's—"

Something nuzzles her ankles. Something soft and warm and insistent. She looks down.

"Oh! Hello there." The F.A.I.R.'s cat couriers are specially chosen for their sleekness and wise judgment. Not every kitten can become one. They must be able to slink through every imaginable place in all sorts of weather—from starlight cyclones to fairy fog. They must also safeguard precious secrets. Which are often much heavier than they seem.

And they have a way of startling Inés at the most awkward moments.

She recognizes this one. A calico. Which means the message she is carrying is both urgent and highly confidential. The cat has visited her several times since she moved into the palace. Inés clasps her hands together at her waist to stop them from shaking.

"This is not the best time," she says, reaching down to scratch behind the cat's ears. Cats like that, don't they? "I hope you can understand."

The cat does not.

She circles Inés's feet even more insistently.

Dalia meows.

"She won't tell you what's in the letter!" Inés straightens and barks back at Dalia. "They are sworn to absolute secrecy. It's all part of the Code of the Courier Cat." That's one thing she can count on, at least.

"I was only saying hello," Dalia says, arching an eyebrow.

"I'll go and get her some water," Floramaria offers. "And a little food. She looks hungry."

"That's quite all right, thank you," Inés replies with a curtsy. She bends down to the cat again. "Would you please take the letter to my room?" She sets her teeth. "I *know* you can find your way there." She's visited often enough.

The cat lifts her paw and bats at Inés's skirt. She's going to tear it. As though Inés needed yet another problem to solve today.

"A calico means an urgent letter," Dalia says. "She's not going to leave until you open it."

Inés glares. "Yes, I know, Dalia. Unlike some so-called princesas, I understand how the palace works."

Fine. She unties the thin ribbon around the cat's neck and unrolls a slender scroll.

She tries to keep calm, but she feels warmth spreading across her cheeks as she reads. Her eyes begin to cloud with impatient tears.

Inés,

As you know, the Bewitched Academy for the Dreadful is a highly selective institution, training only the worst villains. It's not every day we discover a student with your unique talents, and we believe we can help you reach your true potential. We invite you to visit and explore everything the B.A.D. has to offer.

Dreadfully yours,
The B.A.D.

"Is everything all right?" Leonor asks. "You look a little upset." She pushes closer to her.

Inés skitters backward and crumples the scroll in her hand. Another one. Why won't they leave her alone? If anyone finds out about these invitations, she'll have no hope of graduating, let alone being named Fairest of the F.A.I.R. What would her parents say then?

The calico cat slips out the door before Inés can tell her never to come back. Not that it would help.

"Everything is *fine*," Inés says, wishing she had a fan like Profesora Colibrí's to hide behind. She shoves the wadded-up scroll deep into her pocket. "It's an invitation from . . . from . . . the Duquesa of Solimar. Asking me to tea. Again. She won't take no for an answer." Inés shakes her curls from her shoulders. "Unfortunately, the date she has proposed is the same as the ball, so—"

"Why don't you invite her?" Leonor interrupts. "If it means that much to you. Profesora Colibrí put you in charge of invitations. You and Dalia. As a matter of fact, shouldn't you start working on them? Somewhere *else*?"

Invite the duchess. *Not such a bad idea*, Inés thinks. It would show the profesores and princesas how well-connected she is. How desperate people are to be in her company.

If only the duchess actually existed.

CHAPTER 9

The dessert recipes are perfectly interesting. But Dominga wants them to be more than that. She wants them to be unforgettable.

"I still say the phoenix eggs *must* go on the menu," says Princesa Ana-Paula. "Especially if the decorations committee has chosen Mythical Masquerade as a theme."

They would fill the eggs with sweet cream and just a pinch of Dominga's special sugared-glitter firework powder. When guests tapped the chocolate shells open, the eggs would pop with a flurry of sparkle and surprise.

Dominga, Ana-Paula, Jacinta, and Candelaria are sitting in the palace kitchen around the square wooden table that Chef Luís-Esteban usually uses for kneading bread.

"I will have no more explosions in this kitchen!" the chef grumbles. He is standing at the counter, dicing carrots for the evening's dinner.

Jacinta grips the edge of the table. Candelaria and Ana-Paula look as if they are about to dive under it. They aren't used to Chef Luís-Esteban's surly outbursts like Dominga is. She knows by now that he doesn't really mind them using his kitchen as a laboratory. Sometimes he even joins in.

"Don't worry, Chef," Dominga calls back. "I have perfected the formula. No more explosions."

She glances from Ana-Paula to Jacinta to Candelaria. "At least not *very* big ones," she whispers.

Candelaria grins and pulls a jar full of candied nuts from the shelf behind her. She opens it and scoops out a handful.

"What about my idea?" she says, popping a cashew into her mouth. "Sirena salad. With marshmallows and mangoes and white chocolate pearls."

Jacinta nods, taking the jar from Candelaria. "That's what *I* would eat if I were a mermaid," she says. "We should add pineapple too. And seafoam, of course. And maybe some pansies."

Dominga scribbles it all down in her spell book

under the dishes they have already discussed. The phoenix eggs. The pots of whipped dragon fire. The frozen wisps of snow-fairy breath.

"Don't you think that's enough?" Ana-Paula asks.

Dominga closes her spell book and sticks her pencil back in her bun. Perhaps it is enough, but she can't get rid of the itchy feeling that something is missing. Something that will astonish the guests. That will show Mamá that even though Dominga is not the perfect princesa Paloma is, she still has her own extraordinary talents.

And maybe, if she's lucky, the B.A.D. will notice them too.

"Princesas, out of the way," Chef Luís-Esteban shouts. "Rápidamente, por favor." Carrots and onion are simmering on the stove, and he is carrying a giant ball of piecrust to roll out. "I require the table, or there will be no dinner tonight."

Jacinta jumps to her feet. "Of course, Chef," she says.

"Rápidamente," Candelaria repeats, shaking one more palmful of nuts into her hand before tightening the lid over the jar.

Dominga unties the apron she has been wearing and tosses it at the row of hooks by the door. It lands perfectly on an empty one. "We'll meet again next week," she tells the committee, "to finalize the menu."

She hopes by then she will have found the inspiration she is looking for. She hopes she will have heard back from Princesa Perfecta.

"You're not staying to help with the piecrust?" Chef Luís-Esteban asks when he notices Dominga following the others out.

"Not this time."

She can hear the chef muttering as she leaves.

"How am I expected to run a kitchen with such unreliable assistants?" And then the thud of the rolling pin smacking the dough.

Instead of returning to Casita Opal, Dominga goes to the one place she feels sure no one will come looking for her. The chicken coop.

She and Dalia stumbled into it accidentally on one of their first days at the F.A.I.R. The smell alone will keep the other princesas away. And Dalia only goes there if she has a very good reason. The chatter of so many chickens can give a headache to someone who understands animal-speak as well as Dalia does.

Dominga would avoid it too if she didn't need to be absolutely certain that she wouldn't be disturbed.

She leans into the heavy wooden door and

pushes it open. Feathers flutter around her in a sneezy snowstorm. The chickens begin to cluck and rustle.

"Don't worry," she clucks back. "I don't mean to bother you."

She finds a place in a corner that is not too crowded and nestles in with her notebook. She is about to do the unthinkable. The most un-villainous thing she can imagine. Ask for help from Princesa Perfecta.

She opens the spell book and tears out a blank page. She glances around, even though she knows there is no one here but the chickens.

She begins to write.

Dear Perfecta, she begins.

She scratches it out.

She must try to be polite. She starts again.

Dearest Paloma,

I hope everything is awfully splendid back at home. Thank you for the spell book.

She stops. Scratches it out.

Thank you for the diary. It has been surprisingly useful. Now I must ask you for another favor.

"What are you doing?"

"Writing, obviously," Dominga answers without thinking. She is so focused on her letter that it takes her several moments to realize the voice beside her isn't a voice. It is a cluck. From that black-and-white-speckled hen who seems to always find her.

"Well, I can see that," the hen replies. "What I meant was, *what* are you writing?" The hen settles onto Dominga's shoulder. She'll never get rid of her now.

"A letter."

The hen leans over and ruffles her feathers. "A letter? Who is it for?"

Dominga tilts the page so the hen can't read it. *Can* chickens read? She isn't sure, but she doesn't want to risk it.

"Not important," she says. Even though it is. Horribly important.

"Fine, if you don't want to tell me, you don't have to," the hen says in a huff.

"Gracias," Dominga replies, and begins writing again.

"Even though it's awfully rude of you to barge into our home and not even tell us why," the hen continues. "Don't you think, amigas?"

All around the chicken coop, hens begin clucking and flapping and cackling. They won't let up until they have an answer. And Dominga needs to concentrate. She needs to ask Paloma to send her a recipe from the ancient family cookbook. One she has seen nowhere else. One that, when the guests taste it, will make the music fade, the dancing slow, the decorations dissolve into the background.

"If you must know, I'm writing to my sister," Dominga answers. "But it's a secret. You mustn't tell anyone."

She pauses. She wishes she didn't need to say these next three words. Before they leave her mouth, she feels their sting in the pit of her stomach. "Not even Dalia."

CHAPTER
10

In the music salon the next week, Princesa Eloísa sits at the harp, plucking out a melody so gentle and sweet that three canaries flutter in through an open window. They perch on one of the music stands that sprout from the floor like sunflowers. A wood thrush follows them in and settles onto a stack of sheet music, scattering it to the floor.

Even Don Ignacio pokes his head out to

listen until Dalia pushes him back inside her boot. Strictly speaking, no pets are allowed at the F.A.I.R.

Disgusting, Dominga thinks. What a waste of musical talent. Just think how powerful Eloísa could be if she used her musical gifts for bad.

Dalia makes a noise that anyone else might mistake for an old floorboard creaking but that Dominga recognizes at once for flawless possum-speak.

"You still haven't told me what you have planned for the ball," Dalia says. "Something perfectly nauseating, I hope."

Dominga taps her foot on the ground, and not in time with the music. Perhaps her plans for the menu would make Dalia sick. But probably not in the way she expects. Instead of answering,

Dominga points to her ears and then to the harp. *Can't hear you*, she mouths.

The final notes of Eloísa's song float out the window, and the birds chase after them. Princesas Susana, from Casita Sapphire, and Ramira, from Casita Ruby, clap. Eloísa holds her tiara in place with one hand while she bows. She rises again and looks at Dalia.

"Well? What did you think?" she asks, re-fluffing the satin bow at her neck. It got crushed in the midst of her playing. "I wrote it especially to play as our guests arrive. To help them feel welcome and get comfortable here." She looks at the ground. "The palace can be very intimidating when you first arrive."

Comfortable enough to stretch out and take a nap, Dominga thinks. Perhaps that is exactly what

Dalia has in mind. Lull all the guests into an enchanted sleep and then whisper nightmares into their ears that, hard as they try, they can't ever awaken from.

Only, it would be a shame if it happened before they had a chance to sample the food.

"I could join her on the flute," Ramira adds when Dalia doesn't respond. "If you think it needs a little something extra."

"Or the chimes," Susana suggests. She hurries to a stand of gleaming brass tubes, suspended from shortest to longest. She takes the mallet that hangs from the end of the stand and hits three notes in a row. They ring out like the clock tower bells at daybreak.

Dominga can't help it. She yawns. If this was Dalia's plan all along, it's working.

But then a crashing clang jolts her awake.

"I think you ought to try something louder," Dalia says. She presses down on the piano keys again and strikes another chord, this one even more sour than the first. "Something exciting that tells the guests surprises are in store. Something they aren't likely to forget."

Eloísa closes her eyes, as if she is listening to a distant tune that none of the rest of them can hear. She begins to nod along to it. "I think I know what you mean," she says. "Something bolder." She opens her eyes and reaches into a pocket inside her green satin jacket, embroidered with dragonflies and cattails.

She pulls out a small notebook. Dominga's eyes fix on it. A spell book, perhaps? But no. When Eloísa opens the book, Dominga sees that it is lined with musical staffs. Eloísa begins drawing notes and, still staring down at the page, wanders to a window seat to continue composing.

"Make it *loud*," Dominga tells her. "So loud that our guests never fall asleep again." She turns to Dalia and winks.

Carmen appears in the doorway, the rest of the dancing committee crowding in behind her.

"Are you ready to work on the waltz yet?"

Susana steps away from the chimes and sits next to Dalia at the piano. "I've been practicing all week."

Carmen, Pilar, Lizeth, and Marisol push chairs and music stands against the wall, then arrange themselves in the space they cleared. Standing in a circle, each of the princesas raises an arm. Their fingers touch at the center, and Susana begins to play.

"Hold on!" Ramira says, waving her flute. "Shouldn't we wait for Inés?"

Pilar drops her hand. "Inés *did* tell us not to start without her. She wants to approve every step."

Dominga walks to the window. "I'm afraid Inés won't be back for hours," she says, pointing outdoors. "She's gone to gather flowers for the ball."

"The garden isn't far," Marisol says. "How long can it possibly take?"

Dalia and Dominga glance at each other and grin. "Oh, she hasn't gone to the garden," Dalia says, rising from the piano bench and moving to the window to stand beside Dominga.

"I let her borrow one of my sister's maps," Dominga explains. "To help her find some very *special* flowers. It's quite a long walk."

The map isn't Paloma's, and it leads directly into a patch of skunk cabbage.

Carmen picks up the ruffled edge of her gown

and swishes it. "In that case," she says, "let's dance."

Dominga sits balanced on the window ledge and observes the waltz. The princesas turn in a pinwheel for eight counts, then break apart into a line. They stand on tiptoe and flutter forward, then pirouette in perfect unison.

At the end, they dip into low curtsies. "Here's where we'll ask all the guests to join the dance," Marisol says, looking up.

Dominga reaches into her pocket for her spell book and plucks her pencil from her bun. The twirling dancers have given her an idea for a new spiral-shaped cookie. She scribbles a note to herself.

"Another rancid recipe?" Dalia whispers.

Dominga pulls the book closer, so that it nearly touches her nose. "Would you expect anything less?" Then she hops off the window ledge and joins the dancers.

"I liked the spinning," she says. "But there should be *more* of it. And *faster*." She extends her arms and begins to turn, slowly at first, and then so quickly the room becomes a blur.

The dancers watch her and then join in. They spin, faster and faster, until they crash into one another and tumble to the floor.

"Brilliant idea!" Dalia shouts when they look up, dizzy and confused.

Pilar rubs her head. "But I'm afraid some of our guests might become so dizzy they get sick," she says.

"Even better," Dalia mutters, nudging Dominga's shoulder.

"I'm glad you agree," Dominga replies. She doesn't mind what happens to her food *after* the guests have tasted it.

"What was that?" Lizeth asks.

"Never mind," Dalia answers. "I've been thinking more about Pilar's idea to include some animals in the dance."

"Yes!" Pilar says, stumbling to her feet. "Fawns and rabbits."

"More like foxes and rabbits," Dalia says.

Carmen stops in the middle of another pirouette, one hand held over her head. "But won't the foxes chase the rabbits?" she asks. "Won't they try to *eat* them?"

Marisol cries, "Poor bunnies!"

Dalia curls her hands like claws. "But think of the drama!" she growls. Lizeth giggles. She probably thinks Dalia is only joking.

She isn't.

While Dalia chases Marisol around the room, Dominga slips out the door.

CHAPTER 11

Dominga hates to leave the scene of a gruesome animal battle. Even an imaginary one. But she has a secret mission to complete, and Dalia won't be distracted for long. Villains are terribly watchful.

She feels that tight, twisty knot in her stomach again. The one that grows ever more impossibly tangled each time she thinks about the plans she is hiding from Dalia. Each time she adds another recipe to her spell book. Each time she sneaks away or answers Dalia's questions with slippery half-truths. She tells herself that it won't matter—she'll make sure plenty of other dreadful things happen at the ball. After what she just saw in the music salon, she has no doubt that the party is on its way to ruin.

Besides, she thinks, glancing over her shoulder as she winds her way down a silent hallway, *villains are very sneaky.* Who better than Dalia to understand?

Inside the book she gave to Dominga, Paloma sketched a hand-drawn map of the palace, complete with hidden passages, mysterious doors, and unexpected detours. Dominga has never been able to figure out why a princesa as perfect as Paloma would even know such secrets, let alone share them with her.

Perhaps it has something to do with one of the three rules that Paloma inscribed in the book: *A true princesa never loses her way.*

Paloma certainly wouldn't approve of Dominga using the map to get into the B.A.D. But then again, Dominga was never a true princesa.

With everyone busy in class or preparing for the ball, it's easier than usual for her to sneak into the Ruby hallway. Its carpet is woven to look like a field of roses—scarlet and crimson and blush—whose blooms unfold when stepped on.

I must come up with a way to weave in some thorns, Dominga thinks. But it will have to wait.

Rubies glow with the warmth of honor and loyalty, Profesora Colibrí told them. Just like opals flicker with mystery, emeralds promise new beginnings, and sapphires shine with wisdom.

Around a sharp corner and at the end of the hallway is a bookcase that extends from floor to ceiling. Each of the heavy volumes on its shelves records the promises the Ruby princesas have made to themselves and to one another going back all the way to when the F.A.I.R. began.

Dominga double-checks Paloma's map, then tucks her spell book back in her pocket. She takes off her gloves and climbs the bookcase in order to reach its highest shelf. With her fingers, she finds the third volume in and pulls it gently.

She looks down. The roses in the carpet part to reveal a trapdoor. Dominga jumps down from the shelf and opens it.

There are easier ways to get where she needs to go. But this is the most stealthy.

She clambers through the opening, then pulls

the door shut behind her. She creeps through a narrow tunnel, climbs up a rickety ladder, and finally emerges underneath a shaggy rug at the center of the Cattic.

It is the place where the courier cats come to nap and play while they await their next assignments.

"Shhhh." A silky ragdoll cat opens one of his blue eyes and hisses at Dominga.

"I'm sorry for disturbing you," she whispers. "It's only that I'm waiting for a very important message."

The cat closes his eye, stretches, and curls back into a plump feathered cushion. Dominga stands and begins to wander the room. Cats pounce on the pale sunbeams that shine through the skylights. Others doze on quilted beds, tails twitching, or climb the lofty cat towers that stretch toward the rafters.

Dominga imagines Paloma here, holding one of her many letters home. She hopes her older sister has kept up her habit of replying at once to each and every piece of mail. She wants to snag the letter without Dalia seeing.

As Dominga searches for a cat with a scroll bearing Paloma's signature lavender seal, she realizes she is not alone. Amid the purrs and meows, she hears a voice.

"Where are you? I know you have another one. Just give it to me."

Dominga's eyes dart right and left behind her round glasses. She wasn't expecting company. Especially this company.

She follows the voice.

"Inés?"

She finds her crouching in front of a planter filled with catswort, a treat among courier cats. She is pulling back the velvety green leaves and peering inside when a gray paw pokes out and swipes at her nose.

"Ow!" Inés topples backward. Right onto Dominga's boot.

"What are you doing here?" Dominga asks, staring down at her. "I thought you were searching for wildflowers."

What looks like worry flits over Inés's face, but before Dominga is even sure it's there, Inés's confidence returns. She stands and tosses her curls over her shoulder and touches her tiara, which hasn't budged even a fraction of an inch. She reties the ribbon at her waist into a crisp bow, its ends perfectly even.

"Shouldn't you be working on your menu?" Inés

asks. "I expect to taste a sample of each and every dish first thing tomorrow morning."

She didn't answer the question, Dominga thinks. But she doesn't have a chance to ask it again because, just then, a cat with snowy-white fur purrs at her feet. A scroll with a lavender seal is tied to her silver collar.

"Oh, good," Dominga says, kneeling to unfasten the message. "You're right on time." She reaches into her pocket and offers the cat a bit of salmon left over from breakfast as a thank-you. The cat swallows the fish, then trots away to an empty cushion.

Dominga unrolls the message.

"Who is it from?" Inés asks, leaning over to peek.

"My sister," Dominga mumbles, pulling the

letter away from Inés. Her eyes scan the page. *It's here!* she thinks, smiling to herself with relief. *The recipe!*

But Paloma has also left her with a curious message: *You can expect another delivery from Mamá before the ball.*

Her forehead wrinkles. *Why would Paloma mention her letter to Mamá?* Wait. Paloma is a princesa. Of *course* she mentioned it. All the same, what could the delivery be? Nothing good, Dominga is sure.

"From Paloma? I want to see!" Inés reaches for the scroll, nearly tripping on a hairless sphynx cat with piercing eyes and bat-like ears that has just appeared between them. He lifts his head, revealing a message fastened to his collar with black velvet ribbon.

Dominga would recognize that ribbon from miles away. There is only one place the delivery could have come from.

"Why do you have a message from the head villain of the B.A.D.?"

CHAPTER 12

A slap of envy nearly knocks Dominga over. For months, she and Dalia have been hoping to receive their own special delivery from Profesora de la Sombra. But every time they write to tell the academy about their latest schemes and beg to be admitted, all they receive in return is a hastily written reply, sent back with Don Ignacio, telling them they are not yet dreadful enough to attend. Why should Inés, a princesa who's nearly as perfect as Paloma, receive a message from the B.A.D.? And delivered by a sphynx, no less.

Inés's face is as bright red as Dominga has ever seen it. Almost as if some of Chef Luís-Esteban's strawberry syrup had gotten smeared over her cheeks.

Which would have really *made her angry,* Dominga thinks.

Inés crumples the message in her fist and hides it behind her back. "Don't be ridiculous," she says. "Of *course* I haven't received a message from the B.A.D."

Dominga folds Paloma's note into the front cover of her spell book. As much as she'd like to study the recipe now, she must know what's inside Inés's scroll.

"Everyone knows Profesora de la Sombra always binds her messages with bewitched black velvet ribbon," Dominga says, stepping toward Inés. "I'd recognize it anywhere."

Inés sneers. "Of course you would. You could have been friends with me, but you decided to hang out with *Dalia* instead. Even though you know who her mother is."

Dominga takes another step forward. "You admit it's from her, then? Why would she write to *you*?"

Inés backs up into one of the cat trees. It sways dangerously. Dominga lunges to tilt it upright before any of the courier cats fall off. They yowl in complaint.

"It's a mistake," Inés says. "A *terrible* mistake. It has to be."

Dominga scratches the neck of a particularly nervous tabby to calm it. Near Inés's feet, two kittens, couriers-in-training, bat a feather back and forth.

"Maybe I can help," Dominga offers. Perhaps Inés is right. Perhaps it is a mistake. Perhaps, all along, the villains of the B.A.D. have been trying to reach Dalia and Dominga, but somehow their messages have been misdirected to Inés.

And yet, courier cats are so terribly careful.

And the B.A.D. has been perfectly clear: Dalia and Dominga are not villain material.

"Ha!" Inés's laugh comes out like a bark. The cats lift their heads in annoyance. "Help from *you*? A princesa knows how to manage even the most difficult situations. I have this one completely under control. Now, if you'll excuse me, I must be going. There's a ball to plan."

She tries to walk past Dominga.

"But if you'll just let me read it," Dominga says, stretching out her arm.

Inés lifts the letter high above her head where

Dominga can't reach. But instead of going for the letter, Dominga tugs on one of the ends of Inés's ribbon, untying the bow.

The kittens see the ribbon dangle. They jump at it, claws extended.

"No!" Inés cries. She tries to shoo the kittens away, losing hold of the message. Dominga leaps and catches it before it hits the floor. And by the time Inés realizes what has happened, Dominga has read the whole thing.

It is worse than she could have imagined.

Dear Inés,

As you have not yet replied to our many urgent letters, we have become concerned that you have not been receiving them. That is why I have entrusted this delivery to our most capable courier. I believe you have a dark and dreary future at the B.A.D. Please send word at your earliest convenience so that we may prepare your cell.

Dreadfully yours,
Prof. de la Sombra
The B.A.D.

Dominga is so shocked, so astounded, so perplexed that she lets the letter fall, but her hands stay frozen in front of her as if she is still holding it. An invitation to the B.A.D. Sent from the head villain herself. And, apparently, this isn't the first.

"How?" she says, when her words slowly begin to return to her. "Why?"

She and Dalia have been the ones working to

prove themselves worthy villains. They are the ones who have been plotting ever more wicked schemes. Who have dreamed of attending the B.A.D. ever since they first set eyes on its grim and shadowy towers. *They* should be the ones brewing potions alongside the academy's most accomplished witches and caring for creatures inside its monster menagerie.

Not Inés. Who would stop at nothing to be the Fairest of the F.A.I.R. Who would pay any price.

Maybe that's it, Dominga thinks. As their last letter from the B.A.D. said, a true villain never gives up.

And she can't imagine that Inés *ever* would.

"It's silly, really. Just some misunderstanding," Inés says, snatching the message from the cat bed it landed on. She dips it into one of the marble watering fountains, then tears the soggy paper into bits and drops them into a golden litter box.

"There," Inés continues. "As I was saying, it has to be a misunderstanding. Or someone's awful idea of a joke. Either way, I will get to the bottom of it. Just as soon as the ball is over."

The ball.

Of course.

A plot—Dominga's worst yet—begins to hatch. One that will surely inspire Dalia and maybe even the B.A.D.

"About the ball," Dominga begins.

"What about it?" Inés answers. "Are you *finally* ready to help?"

"I am. But Dalia and I have some ideas that you don't seem to agree with."

Inés crosses her arms and flutters her eyelashes.

"Of course not. How could I? Your ideas have been dreadful. We want our guests to *enjoy* themselves. With a sister like Paloma, I'm surprised you don't understand. I'm surprised you don't *care*."

Dominga glances down at the kittens, preparing once again to jump for Inés's ribbon. "I happen to think our ideas are perfect, and you should go along with them. *All* of them. Unless . . ."

Inés narrows her eyes. "Unless what?"

Dominga tilts her chin toward the litter box. "Unless you want the whole school—even Profesora Colibrí—to know that the B.A.D. has been recruiting you. That they believe you have villain potential."

Inés gasps. She holds her fingers, nails painted carnation pink, to her mouth. "You wouldn't dare! I'll tell everyone about Dalia's mom! You'll be kicked out of the F.A.I.R. for certain."

"Doesn't matter," Dominga says. "We're not planning to stay anyway." There's someplace else they want to go. Someplace bleaker.

Inés sniffs. "No one will believe you."

Dominga shrugs. "Maybe not at first," she says. "But don't you think, in the backs of their minds, they'll wonder whether it's true? I suppose we'll find out." She turns to leave.

And then, just as Dominga knew she would, Inés yells, "Wait!"

CHAPTER 13

The princesas have swept every crumb and speck of dust off the floors of the Great Hall so that the tiles gleam like jewels. They scrub the windows until they sparkle. They polish the banquet tables until the deep brown wood seems to glow.

Dominga sits on one of the tabletops and closes her eyes. She imagines herself surrounded by her dishes, steaming and savory and sweet, as guests run wildly in fright and confusion. Because now there's no way the ball will turn out like the schemes she and Dalia have planned before. The party can only be a disaster.

"And over here is where I thought we could build the dragon's cave," Leonor explains, moving toward the stone fireplace. "Since it's already full of ashes and smells like burnt tortillas."

Dalia sticks her head inside and sniffs the air. "Yes, but not burnt enough," she says, brushing soot off her nose.

Dominga opens her eyes and hops off the table. She pulls two hard-boiled eggs from her pocket. "Here," she says, presenting the eggs to Leonor, who grimaces at the smell. "They're overcooked. The menu committee will boil up a whole potful for you."

Leonor sets the eggs down and glances back at

Inés. She is sitting at a table toward the back of the hall, hand-writing invitations to send down to the village.

"You're not going to say anything, Inés?" Leonor asks. "About the eggs? Really?"

Inés looks up. She grinds her teeth. "No," she says sharply. "Overcooked egg sounds *awfully* nice." She squeezes the quill she is holding so tightly that it snaps in half. It must be the third one she's broken this morning, if Dominga is counting correctly. But Inés doesn't protest. She can't. Dominga has made sure of that.

Instead, Inés smiles and opens a carved wooden box. She selects a new feather, this one frilly and creamy white, and dips it into a pot filled with shimmering silver ink.

"All right, then," Leonor says, adding some notes to her sketch pad. "Overcooked eggs it is.

I have to admit, these decorations aren't anything like what I was expecting, but I love having the chance to try something new. I've worked with charcoal before, but never ashes and flame."

Valentina waves down from a ladder that reaches the rafters. Looped over her arm is a bundle of vines, grayish green and slimy. "Up here is where we'll hang tendrils of algae for the lake monster's lair."

Dalia shakes her hair out of her eyes and gazes at the ceiling. "Do you think some of the moss and algae could sort of drip down?" she asks. She mimes the drip-dropping with her fingers.

"Like this?" Valentina pulls a single leaf off the vine and lets it flutter to the floor.

"Ugh!" Inés pushes herself away from the table. "Do I have to do everything around here?"

She stomps over to the ladder. "Off!" she shouts

at Valentina. Once Valentina has climbed down, Inés yanks away the vines and climbs the ladder herself. When she gets to the top, she tears off a handful of leaves, mashes them in her hand, then flings them. They land on the tile with a wet splat. "Like that," she says, grinning as she hops back to the floor.

Perhaps she has villain potential after all, Dominga thinks with a shudder. Or maybe it's only that Inés can't keep herself from ordering everyone around. Even if it means ordering them to create the ball of her nightmares.

Dalia nods. "Yes, exactly," she says warily. "Like that. And perhaps some slime bubbles?"

"Oh!" Dominga has already thought of that. She reaches for her spell book. "I have the perfect recipe for slime."

Floramaria looks up at the rafters and squints.

"But back to the algae," she says. "Aren't you worried it might land on our guests? What if it falls in their eyes? Or stains their clothes?"

"Even better!" Dalia says. "Then our guests will feel they are truly trapped in—that is, truly *a part of*—the world you've created."

Just outside, in the palace entryway, Eloísa is blowing into a trumpet. At least Dominga assumes it is a trumpet. Judging by the sound alone, it could be an angry elephant. One that also happens to be suffering from a head cold.

"Sorry about that!" Eloísa yells. "I'm still learning, but I pick up new instruments very quickly. It will sound much better by the time the ball is here."

Hopefully not, Dominga thinks.

Eloísa blows out another thunderously sour

note. The windows rattle, and this time, Susana joins her on the violin.

"Stop!" Dalia says. "It's all wrong." She hurries to her satchel, resting under one of the tables, and returns with an ancient violin. She and Dominga found it stashed in one of the hidden tunnels on Paloma's map. "Try this."

Susana stares down at the instrument, which is dented and caked with dust. Inés leans over and snaps one of its strings.

"If you say so," Susana says. She brings the violin to her shoulder.

When Dominga hears the sound it makes, she wonders for a moment if the courier cats are howling in protest of their workload again.

"Are you sure I shouldn't just play my own violin?" Susana asks.

"Trust me," Dalia says. "It is magnificent."

Leonor rubs her temples. "I think I'll wait to hear the music at the ball. I need to work on the Minotaur maze anyway."

Inés follows her outside. "I better help. You might not make it twisty enough."

Then, while Valentina and Floramaria continue working on the lake monster's lair, Dalia and Dominga wander back to the table where Inés has left the invitations.

"Looks like she's inviting the whole village," Dominga notes, looking at the stack of delicate paper.

"Good," Dalia says. "We don't want anyone to miss this." She pauses. "Do you think Inés is up to something? It almost seems like she's *helping* us all of a sudden."

Dominga has not yet revealed the true reason

behind Inés's change of heart. She'll explain everything to Dalia at the ball. When she tells her how she orchestrated the entire scheme. The surprise will be far more delicious if she waits till then. Dalia will be so shocked, she'll hardly notice that Dominga failed to spoil the feast.

"You're not worried, are you?" Dominga asks, avoiding an answer.

"Of course not," Dalia says. "Even if she changes our decorations or replaces the musicians or teaches a new dance, she won't be able to stop you from sabotaging the meal."

Dominga pats her pocket, reassuring herself that her recipe, sent straight from Paloma, is still safe inside her spell book. She has gathered nearly all the ingredients.

"In fact," Dalia goes on, "I am so certain this ball is going to be the most horrific debacle the

F.A.I.R. has ever witnessed, I am going to invite some very special guests."

She pulls a blank invitation off Inés's stack. She borrows the pencil Dominga always keeps tucked in her bun and begins to write.

She addresses the invitation to the Bewitched Academy for the Dreadful.

"This way," she says, still scribbling, "they can see for themselves how wicked we are."

CHAPTER 14

It is the afternoon of the ball. Dominga looks down at the box that arrived early in the morning, dragged in by a team of four courier cats. She recognizes her mother's handwriting on the front.

The rest of the Opal princesas have already gotten dressed and gone down to the grand entrance to await their guests. Dominga is running behind because she needed to put finishing touches on her dish. She was about to change into one of her usual mud-colored gowns when she remembered she hadn't opened Mamá's package.

She lifts the lid and recognizes the thin blue tissue paper that Mamá's dressmaker wraps all his designs in. She frowns. But then she tears through the paper and sees what's underneath.

Instead of the frilly and frothy gown she expected Mamá to send—something Paloma might keep in her closet—she finds shadow-gray tulle and satin that looks almost like a puff of smoke from a potion bottle. Or like the ashes a phoenix rises from—especially when Dominga lifts the gown out of the box, holds it to her chest, and notices the red spangles at the bottom, glowing like embers.

A note falls from the dress's many layers of fabric.

Dominga,

This is not at all what I would have ordered for you, but Paloma said it would be perfect. In fact, she insisted. I hope your first ball at the F.A.I.R. convinces you to leave behind all thoughts of villains and trickery for good.

As ever,
Mamá

Paloma is responsible for this dress? A dress Dominga actually *wants* to wear? The idea is as perplexing as the mystery of why Paloma gave Dominga a secret map of the palace. She feels a brief burst of excitement. But Dominga cannot stop to figure it out. She has barely enough time to scramble into the dress and join the rest of the princesas before the doors open.

She is still pulling on her gloves, as light as ash, when she gets to the grand entrance. She almost stumbles when she sees the gowns. Many princesas are dressed as mermaids, their skirts covered in sequins that glint like scales. One is a griffin, with wings made of shimmering silk feathers. And she has never seen so many unicorns.

Dominga spots Dalia amid a herd of them. She hurries toward her.

"I was worried you'd miss it," Dalia says. She wears a gown made of midnight blue velvet with buttons running up to her neck. A swarm of black widow spiders seems to be marching from her waist to her shoulder.

"Miss the moment when our greatest scheme unfolds?" Dominga says, lowering her voice, even though the chatter of all the princesas is loud enough to mask anything they say. "When we finally get the attention of the B.A.D.? *Never.*"

Profesora Colibrí flits her way through the crowd in a purple ball gown alive with twinkling firefly lights. Flowers burst from her fan whenever she waves it, perfuming the air as they tumble to the floor and vanish.

"For several weeks now, the first-year princesas have worked to prepare a ball, not for themselves but for the community," she says. "Now, in the spirit of bienvenida—"

"Profesora, if I may say a few words." Inés has jostled her way to the front. Her gown looks like a daffodil, ivory on top with a skirt that sways like pale yellow petals. "As Reina de la Fiesta—"

"Co-reina!" someone interrupts.

Profesora Colibrí places a hand on Inés's shoulder. "We have kept our guests waiting long enough, don't you agree?"

Before Inés can answer, Profesora Colibrí waves her fan. Roses and orchids spill over the top of it as the doors creak open.

"Now!" Dalia shouts.

Eloísa calls out, "Uno, dos, tres," and as the guests pour in, the music committee begins to play.

Dalia and Dominga look at each other. It's not the clanging, clashing noise they heard a few days ago. Now Eloísa's trumpet is smooth and mellow. Susana's violin has been repaired, and its notes ripple out like a stream. Ramira keeps the rhythm on a deep-voiced guitarrón.

"Much better!" Inés cries.

"*So* much worse," Dominga groans. What could have gone so *right*?

Dalia dashes around skirts and steps over satin slippers to get to Eloísa. "I thought you couldn't play the trumpet!"

Eloísa points to Ramira, who takes over the melody. "I told you not to worry," she says with a wink. "I'm a very fast learner." She lifts her horn back to her mouth.

Dalia takes a breath as though she is about to protest, but a scream from inside the Great Hall distracts her.

Then there's another.

"The decorations!" Dominga says, relief brightening her voice. "The guests must be terrified!"

They link arms and rush inside. But they do not find frightened party guests. Instead, children dance underneath the lake monster, trying to catch slime bubbles on their fingertips and squealing in glee every time a glob of algae lands on their heads.

"I didn't want to make you two feel bad, but I didn't think anyone would actually *like* that," Leonor admits. She tilts back in her chair and spins. She is dressed as a candle sprite in layers of orange silk and flickering crystals. "But you were right! They're having fun. Almost as much fun as we had creating it."

Near the fireplace, princesas giggle as they leap over the dragon fire that roars out every few minutes. "It wasn't supposed to be a game," Dalia says, her jaw clenched. "It was supposed to be a catastrophe."

Dominga's heart races. She remembers another one of the rules Paloma inscribed in her book. *A* true *princesa* makes the most of every situation. She and Dalia should have seen this coming.

"*Someone* suggested wildflowers." Inés's voice rises above the noise of the party. "But as Reina de la Fiesta, I had to stand firm. We couldn't settle for any ordinary theme. We wanted something dazzling. Something *different*."

Dalia and Dominga search the crowd, desperate to find someone who isn't having a terribly wonderful time.

"There!" Dominga says, pointing to a girl from the village. Her nose is running, and her cheeks are pink and blotchy. She wipes away a tear.

"Pitiful," Dalia agrees, a smile beginning to curl the corners of her mouth.

But then Carmen takes the girl by the finger and leads her to the dance floor. She gives her a sparkling phoenix feather, and the girl begins to laugh.

Dalia slumps down onto a chair. "Perfect," she mutters. "Why is everything always so perfect around here?"

Dominga can feel her heart thudding in her ears now. She should have spent more time plotting. She shouldn't have planned such a scrumptious feast. Perhaps, if she hurries, she can still race back to the kitchen and ruin it.

"At least," Dalia says, "no one from the B.A.D. showed up. I thought—I hoped—they might come. But I would hate for them to see *this*."

Then, suddenly, the music crashes to a halt. The dancers freeze in their steps. Inés screeches. "Who invited *them*?"

CHAPTER
15

Dalia grabs Dominga by the elbow and pulls her toward the entrance and what seems to be the source of all the commotion. They find everyone staring at the three latest guests to arrive. They're dressed in long gray robes—the most spectacular Dominga has ever seen—that seem to float above the floor. One wears a spider-silk veil over her eyes. Another has electric-green gloves that stretch over her elbows like twin pythons swallowing her arms. The third and tallest wears a small glass vial around her neck. It is filled with a bubbling, burbling liquid that one moment glows purple and the next deep red. A teleportation potion. Dominga almost rushes forward to ask how to brew it.

She stops herself. She hisses in turkey vulture, "Do you think they're from—"

"The B.A.D.," Dalia hisses back. "Yes, I am certain of it."

The villain with the potion bottle straightens her neck so that she stands even taller. "That's right, we have come from the B.A.D.," she says, eyes darting around the room, as if she is trying to discover where the hisses—flawless turkey vulture, Dominga is proud to note—came from.

"Well, you can turn around and go straight back there," Inés says, dangling a butterscotch-yellow handkerchief in front of her face. She doesn't want the new guests to recognize her, Dominga realizes.

The villains huddle and whisper to themselves. Dominga strains to listen but hears nothing but the squeaky babble of bats. The trio must have placed a voice-cloaking enchantment over themselves. Very clever. Very tricky. She realizes her mouth has fallen open.

Eventually, the one with the spider veil raises her head. Violet ringlets spill over her shoulders. "If you didn't want us to attend, then why did you invite us?"

"*Invite* you?" Inés snaps her handkerchief, no longer concerned about concealing her face. "Don't be ridiculous. Who would do that?"

This is their moment, Dominga thinks. She and Dalia turn to each other and smile. *Wickedly*,

Dominga hopes. She steps forward. "We—" she starts to proclaim.

But before she can finish, Profesora Colibrí steps in front of them all and flutters her fan.

"Princesas," she says, "let us remember our manners."

Inés stiffens, then curtsies—barely a bob of her head—and ducks back into the crowd.

Profesora Colibrí nods and turns to the trio from the B.A.D. Dominga holds her breath.

"You are most welcome to the Fine and Ancient Institute for the Royal," the profesora says. "Por favor, make yourselves comfortable."

Arms laced, the three of them stride into the Great Hall.

"Quick!" Dalia shouts. "Bring out Dominga's dish! Now!"

Her dish? No! Dominga's stomach flips when she realizes what is about to happen.

"I'll go get it!" Ana-Paula says, already sprinting toward the kitchen.

"I'll help!" Jacinta yells, just as eager to get away.

Dominga starts after them. "Wait! The timing . . . It's all wrong!"

But Dalia stops her. "It's our only chance," she says, leading Dominga back to the Great Hall. "Everything has turned out to be so disgustingly delightful. Your dish is all we have left to spoil the ball. To show the villains, in front of all these people, that we belong with *them*."

"But you don't understand," Dominga pleads. She is trotting after Dalia, but still trying to pull away. "There's something I have to explain."

It is too late.

Jacinta and Ana-Paula have returned, each of them lifting a handle on either side of a steaming cauldron. Dalia races ahead to a table at the center of the room. She stands on top of it, eyes glittering. "Bring it here." She beckons to Jacinta and Ana-Paula.

Dominga tries to get to her. To stop her. But the crowd has become too thick, and she can't push through.

"It is time for the greatest surprise of the evening," Dalia announces.

Candelaria wheels out a cart with crystal goblets and a silver ladle. She hands the ladle to Dalia, who dips it into the cauldron and scoops up a serving of thick brownish goo.

Dominga can hardly stand to watch.

Leonor scrunches her nose. "*That's* the special recipe? What *is* it?"

Dalia hands her a goblet and a spoon. "Have a taste," she says. "Have two."

But before Leonor can accept it, Inés steps in and pulls the cup away. "Not so fast," she says. "I'd better taste it first. Quality control. I told Dominga I needed to sample *everything*."

Dalia arches an eyebrow. She glances at Dominga, but Dominga turns away.

"Por favor," Dominga hears Dalia say with oozing generosity. "Be my guest."

Then, with everyone watching, Inés drops her spoon into the sludge. She lifts a small glob of it to her lips. She takes a bite. She closes her eyes.

For one long moment, it's still possible that the dessert will make Inés gag. That it's gone rancid somehow. That Dominga mistook the spicy horseradish sauce for sweet cream again.

But then Inés's amber-brown eyes pop open.

"Delicious." She blinks as if she can't quite believe it.

Dominga doesn't know what happens next because, before she can find out, she shoves her way out of the hall, down a dim corridor, and into a grandfather clock that disguises still another secret passageway that Paloma so bafflingly-yet-helpfully drew on her map.

Dominga thought it would be worth it to dazzle the guests with her cooking. And now Inés, the pickiest princesa of all, has called her dish delicious.

She should be monstrously proud. Instead she is miserable.

Yet again, she has failed to prove herself a true villain. Even worse, she has betrayed her best friend. Dalia was counting on her, and she let her down. In front of everyone.

She creeps to a cobwebby corner and slides down against the wall. Her dress is probably covered in dust and grime now. Mamá would be furious.

Not even *that* makes Dominga feel any better.

She wants to be alone. She wants to be invisible. But because this evening seems to only get worse (and not in a good way), Dominga hears footsteps approaching. Probably that hen again.

"Go away," Dominga clucks, hugging her knees to her chest. "You'll have more fun at the party. There should be plenty of crumbs."

"I've never had fun at a party," Dalia says.

Dominga lifts her eyes and pushes her glasses back up the bridge of her nose. Dalia doesn't look happy. But she doesn't look especially *unhappy* either.

And she is carrying two goblets of Dominga's flan. She offers her one.

"It makes me sick just to look at it," Dominga whimpers.

"What happened?" Dalia asks. Behind her dark curls, her eyes are wide and confused.

"I don't know," Dominga replies. "I guess I actually like working in Chef Luís-Esteban's kitchen?" It is difficult to admit out loud. "And I wanted to show everyone that I'm terribly good at something. With all the other schemes we had planned, I didn't think the food would matter. But then . . ."

Dalia pours Dominga's serving of custard into her own goblet. "Why didn't you tell me?" she asks, sitting beside her.

"Because we're *supposed* to be villains," Dominga says.

"Exactly," Dalia replies. "And villains make their own rules. If you want to make potions *and* desserts, no one can stop you."

Dominga takes the extra spoon and dips it into Dalia's goblet. The flan is as good as she hoped it would be. Which isn't so bad after all.

CHAPTER 16

From one of the palace's many balconies, Dalia and Dominga watch the three guests from the B.A.D. slink away into the night.

"They didn't stay for Eloísa's big finale," Dominga observes, swallowing the last spoonful of her third helping of flan.

"And they didn't attempt Leonor's labyrinth," Dalia adds, scraping up what's left of hers.

Neither of them says what else they are thinking, which is, *They didn't even ask us to come with them.*

When the villains are barely specks in the moonlight, Dalia speaks again. "I wonder what they will report when they get back to the B.A.D."

Unfortunately, Dominga can already imagine it.

"Good. They're finally gone."

Dalia and Dominga turn and find Inés behind them, scowling at the horizon. "I thought they'd never leave." She keeps watching, even after the villains are no longer visible, as if she doesn't trust that they won't try to come back. Her daffodil dress looks dull and wilted.

The sounds of muffled music and distant laughter drift up from the ball downstairs. And every few minutes, they hear a pop and squeal that tells them someone has tapped open another one of Ana-Paula's phoenix eggs.

The sky dims to a dark, starry indigo.

"There you are," Profesora Colibrí chirps, coming up behind them. "Just the princesas I have been looking for."

"Profesora!" Inés presses a hand to her heart. "I want you to know that I had *nothing* to do with what happened here—"

Profesora Colibrí flutters her fan, sending up swirls of feathery pink peonies. Inés blinks and waves them away.

"As I was saying," Profesora Colibrí continues. "You are just the princesas I have been looking for. Princesa Dalia and Princesa Inés, I commend you for a royally original ball. You gave your classmates a chance to let their talents shine. And, most importantly, you made sure that all of our guests would feel welcome, no matter where they come from." She pauses and gazes out toward the towers of the B.A.D.

She drops her long fingers on Dalia's shoulder and squeezes. "It's what your mother would have done . . . when she was Fairest of the F.A.I.R."

Inés opens her mouth as if she's about to argue, or possibly to scream. But all that comes out is a small, pinched squeak.

Dalia and Dominga agree that whatever they think at the B.A.D., the whole evening was worth it, just for the look on Inés's face.

Though, if Dominga is being honest, Dalia looked just as appalled.

Now that the shock has begun to wear off, they race back to the Great Hall, determined to throw a dash of Dominga's firework powder into the dragon's lair.

"Perhaps we could start our *own* school for villains someday," Dominga says, raising her voice above the roar of the exploding dragon's breath.

They back away and return to the buffet table.

"Why not now?" Dalia asks, holding Don Ignacio over the edge of the punch bowl so that he can take a drink. "Right under their noses."

Dominga can already imagine the havoc. She reaches for her notebook, ready to begin writing down ideas. But despite the fact that she has no intention of having *fun* at this horrid ball, she can't help but sway along to the beat of Eloísa's music.

Dalia, she notices, is tapping a toe.

"It couldn't hurt," Dominga says, pointing to the dance floor.

"Not after everything else that's gone wrong tonight," Dalia agrees.

Together, they begin to spin with the other princesas and villagers, faster and faster, until the ballroom is all a blur.

"This is amazing!" Marisol shouts, taking both their hands. "When Profesora Colibrí asks who contributed most to the ball, I'm voting for the two of you!"

Dominga can't keep up anymore. She drops Marisol's hand and twirls off the dance floor.

Dalia joins her, clutching her stomach. "Everyone has eaten quite a lot tonight," she says.

"An *awful* lot," Dominga agrees.

"Wouldn't it be terrible if the dancing *does* make them sick?"

"Perfectly terrible," Dominga replies, feeling

slightly queasy herself. "We should stay and watch. Just in case."

At the far end of the dance floor, Inés shrieks. "Get away from me! I told you I didn't want to see you again! I'm not the one you're looking for!"

She stomps away and runs out the door.

"But, Inés," Leonor shouts after her. "It's only a courier cat. What are you so upset about?"

Princesas and villagers smile and coo as the cat trots across the dance floor. Some bend to pet him, but the cat doesn't stop. Couriers are terribly focused when on duty. He charges ahead until he finds Dalia and Dominga.

Dominga has to squint in the dim light to see that it's the same sphynx from the other day in the Cattic.

"You again," she says. "If you're looking for Inés,

she's run away. You'll have to find her in her suite. Over there." She points.

"*Again?*" Dalia asks. "You've seen this cat before?"

Of course. In all the chaos of the unraveling ball, she forgot to tell Dalia about Inés's secret messages.

"You'll never believe it," she begins. But then she stops. She notices that the cat hasn't moved. His blue eyes glimmer in the lantern light. He bats at the spangles on Dominga's skirt.

"Maybe the letter is for you," Dalia says.

The sphynx meows. Very refined cat-speak for, "Both of you, in fact." He bows his head and reveals a scroll, neatly tied with a piece of black velvet ribbon.

"For us?" Dalia asks.

"Are you sure?" Dominga adds.

The cat purrs, then impatiently flicks his tail.

Dominga kneels to unfasten the message. Together, she and Dalia carry it to a dark corner to read.

To Dalia and Dominga,

We admit we were aghast to learn that any aspiring villain would agree to plan a ball. For princesas, no less. Most un-wicked. However, our spies have returned with reports that at least *some* of the festivities were pleasingly putrid. We may even steal an idea or two for our own Ball for the Banished. With improvements, naturally. It seems you have a shred of villain potential after all.

Or perhaps it was just good luck. We cannot yet say for certain. So, for now, you must remain at the F.A.I.R. We invite you to keep trying . . . and to convince your friend Inés to reply to our letters.

Awfully yours,
The B.A.D.

See how it all began in

BAD PRINCESSES:

PERFECT VILLAINS

It is a glittery-golden morning on the first day of school for royalty in training.

Ghastly golden, if you ask Princesa Dominga. She grimaces at the parade of princesas that jostle past her, jewel-toned traveling cloaks billowing over their shoulders as they hurry toward the grand arched entry to the palace.

Dominga tightens her own cloak around her neck, as though she could make herself disappear behind its black velvet folds. Already, the Fine and Ancient Institute for the Royal is far worse than she ever could have predicted. She should have jumped from her mother's carriage the moment she realized where it was taking her.

She squints into the dazzling sun and wishes she were someplace dark. Someplace dank. Someplace *else*. She closes her eyes and imagines it. She can almost smell the mold and mildew. She can nearly hear the steady *drip drip drip* of sludge down a dungeon wall.

But as soon as she opens her eyes, the scene dissolves. Faster than a nightmare at daybreak.

There is no escape. The last carriages clatter away after late-arriving princesas have said their goodbyes, and the gates clang shut behind them. Dominga's mamá stayed only long enough leave her with a warning: "If I hear any more of this villain nonsense, I'll yank you back to the castle, where you'll spend your days managing Paloma's correspondence." Princesa Paloma—more like *Princesa Perfecta*—is Dominga's older sister. She graduated from the F.A.I.R. the year before and would one day be queen.

If there is anything more appalling than the F.A.I.R., it is the thought of being stuck at home, writing Paloma's letters. Would she have to sign them with the same flourish of hearts and flowers that her sister did? Better to never find out.

Dominga supposes she is stuck. For now. She looks past the locked gate where, no more than a day's walk away, the Bewitched Academy for the Dreadful is perched atop a grim and craggy cliff. Storm clouds as dark as shadows swirl around its spindly towers.

That *is where I should be*, Dominga thinks. That *is where I belong.*

About the Author

JENNIFER TORRES is the award-winning author of the Bad Princesses series; *The Do-Over*; *The Win Over*; *Stef Soto, Taco Queen*; and many other books for young readers. She writes stories about home, friendship, and unexpected courage inspired by her Mexican American heritage. Jennifer started her career as a newspaper reporter, and even though she writes fiction now, she hopes her stories still have some truth in them. She lives with her family in Southern California.